# The Laziest Man in the World

## A Comedy in One Act

by Carl Webster Pierce

A SAMUEL FRENCH ACTING EDITION

## CHARACTERS

JIM  
BILL } *two burglars.*  
MR. HEMIT, *their host.*  
BENSON, *a servant.*

SCENE: *A room in* MR HEMIT'S *apartment, early in the evening.*

*Playing time about twenty-five minutes.*

# The Laziest Man In The World

SCENE: *A room in* HEMIT'S *apartment. The entrance is* C *, by a double doorway with practical doors. There are two windows at the left, hung with long draperies. Down right, against the wall, is a small safe. In the upper right corner is a screen, and near it is a music rack. Left center is a library table, with a drawer facing left. On the table is a wooden box about a foot long; and a telephone on an extension arm is attached to right side of table. At left of table is an armchair Just to the left of the door is a small table with ash-tray, matches, newspaper, magazines and a cigar. The room is elegantly furnished. Several candelabra are on the walls, and a handsome electric dome hangs just to the right of the table. The light switch is just to the right of the door.*

*(As the curtain rises the room is illuminated by the soft light of the hanging lamp only. A faint glow enters through the windows. The doors are shut.* BILL *leans lazily against the casement of the lower window, staring out. He is lazy even in his speech* JIM *is on his knees before the safe, industriously working with a hand-drill; various tools are scattered around him. He is of a quick-spoken, nervous type; the very opposite of* BILL. *He stops and looks at the drill.)*

JIM.   Damn!
BILL.   Huh?
JIM.   Bit's hot.
BILL.   Stick it in the oil.
JIM.   *(Contemplating the safe)*   Tough tin in this can.
BILL.   Yeh.
JIM.   Two bits broke already.
BILL.   Let this one cool.  Rest awhile.
JIM.   *(Inspecting with a flashlight)*   Point's dulled.
BILL.   Rest up a minute and it won't seem so.
JIM.   Ain't tired, Bill   Besides, I can rest better after I'm out o' here.   *(He starts to drill again.)*
BILL.   You're a demon for work.
JIM.   I want to get somewheres.
BILL.   No hurry; take it easy.
JIM.   *(Rising and stretching)*   Gee, I'm cramped.
BILL.   *(Turning from the window)*   Wouldn't be if you'd listen to me.   Drill five minutes and then rest ten.
JIM.   Why don't you drill awhile?
BILL.   Ain't I lookout on this job?   Didn't I crack the last one?
JIM.   No, you didn't.   You was supposed to, but I did most of it.
BILL.   Didn't have to.   I'd 'a' got it done if you'd let me take my time.
JIM.   You wouldn't 'a' been through yet.   You're lazier'n a cold fly, Bill.
BILL.   I won't work myself to death for anyone.
JIM.   If you don't turn more energetic, I'll have to bust up our combine.   It makes me nervous.
BILL.   You don't need to get nervous.   I'm a-watchin' out.
JIM.   *(Scornfully)*   Bah!   I don't mean that I'm afraid.   It's havin' you 'round my neck useless like

what upsets me.   Like a kid always runnin' under its mother's feet

BILL.   Don't complain; drill   The bit's cooled now.   *(He again leans against the window.)*   I'm a-standin' guard.

JIM.   Yes, you are!   The window's safe.   There ain't no fire-escape there.   Why don't you lean against the door for a change?

BILL.   I can hear 'em comin' from here   I like to look out o' the window.

JIM.   *(At work)*   What you lookin' at?

BILL.   *(Dreamily)*   The stars and the lights o' the city.   'Bout a million of each, I guess   *(He sighs.)*

JIM.   What's the matter?   Tired o' loafin'?

BILL.   Nope.   I'm a-wishin'.

JIM.   What?

BILL.   That they was a dollar in that safe for every star I can see.

JIM.   Maybe they is.   *(Disgusted)*   But you'd never find out if it wasn't for me.

BILL.   Would, too.

JIM.   *(Laboriously turning the drill)*   You'd die —of old age—before you ever got through this

BILL.   I wouldn't do it that way.

JIM.   Huh!   *(Inspects his work with the flashlight.)*   S'pose you'd ask the servant to bring the combination.

BILL.   I'd soup it and save time.

JIM.   That'd be sense!

BILL.   Wha' d'ye say, let's soup it.

JIM.   Yeh!   Five stories o' people under us, and two over.   They wouldn't hear no explosion; they're all deaf, I don't think!   Bill, I believe your laziness is turnin' you crazy.

BILL.   We could muffle it.   Look at these hangin's and the rugs.

JIM.  We'll carry it out the way we planned.  *(A sharp click is heard.)*

BILL.  *(Showing interest)*  Are you through?

JIM   Nope.  Another bit busted.  *(He inserts a new one.)*

BILL.  *(Settling back against the window)*  Oh. Tough baby, ain't it?  Gettin' tired?

JIM.  Nope.

BILL.  All right.  *(Doubtfully)*  If you *want* to watch, I *could* drill awhile

JIM   Nope

BILL   *(With a sigh of relief)*  All right.  Thought you was gettin' tired, maybe.

JIM   I won't be tired enough to quit until we're through.

BILL   I'd never work hard enough to get tired.

JIM   Bill, I believe you are the laziest man in the world!  A gentleman in our profession can take it easy between times, but when a job is bein' tackled he ought to have plenty of pep.

BILL.  Huh!

JIM.  Sometime you are goin' to get nabbed—and just because you are so cussed lazy.

BILL   D'ye know, Jim, I've sometimes thought about lettin' myself be caught—on a small job, so's I wouldn't get too long a stretch

JIM.  *(In amazement)*  What's eatin' you?

BILL   A few weeks would be a nice vacation; steady place to sleep, three meals a day, and no business worries.  Gosh, I'd like a rest

JIM.  Rest?  I'd think you'd be tired o' doin' nothin'; and that's all you've done since we teamed up

BILL   *(Resentfully)*  Zat so?  Who got the dope on this place?

JIM.  It was a tough thing to do, wasn't it?  You get to talkin' to a housemaid in the park—where you was loafin'—and grab off some gossip she got from the coot who works here.  And then you claim that you did a wonderful job in smellin' out this here crib.

BILL.   Aw, Jim, ain't it been tough to stay in that room across the street every evenin' for a week? *(Points out of window.)*

JIM.   Yeh!   That was tough, it was!   Parkin' your lazy carcass in a ten dollar a day hotel   Did you want someone to hold the field glasses to your eyes while you rubbered over here to get the dope?

BILL.   It was monotonous work

JIM.   Yeh   Maybe you went to sleep on it.   Are you sure you got things straight?

BILL.   Couldn't 'a' slipped.   The windows was wide open every night, and I saw the whole works

JIM.   You're sure the old boy is paralyzed so he can't walk?

BILL   Ain't I seen him wheeled into this here room on a regular dolled-up operatin'-table every night for a week?   From his hips down he's as helpless as if he was under six foot o' sod.

JIM.   Are you sure the feller what wheels him in goes out?

BILL   How many times are you goin' to put me through the third degree?

JIM.   I want to get the dope straight.

BILL.   Well, I'm tellin' you that the young feller goes out every evening.   I've watched 'till he turned the corner every night.

JIM.   You're sure the old boy has plenty of cash in here?   *(Indicates the safe )*

BILL.   Sure.

JIM.   Maybe that Jane in the park was talkin' big just to make you think she had a head full o' knowledge.

BILL   She chattered true, all right   Besides, I've seen him take a roll of bills big enough to choke a cow out o' that tin can.   *(Sighs )*   Through the glasses I could even see the century mark on 'em

He keeps a lot o' good-lookin' sparklers in there, too.

JIM  *(Rises and stretches, then crosses and gazes out of window)*  You must have good eyesight to see all that from over there

BILL.  Those were powerful glasses you got me.

JIM.  *(Proudly)*  They was the best which was in stock at the leadin' jeweller's at two A.M. the mornin' after we planned this.

BILL  *(With a chuckle)*  Seen in the paper to-day that Mr. Jeweller collected his burglar insurance O. K

JIM.  That's good.  I wouldn't want 'em to lose on our account.  Well, I must get back to work.

BILL.  For heaven's sake, don't kill yourself workin'.

JIM  But we must get through as soon as possible.

BILL.  'Nother hour'll finish it.

JIM.  Less 'n that.

BILL.  It's 'bout time for Mr. cripple to be rolled in.

JIM  It will be more cheerful-like to have some one to chat with.  You're too busy moonin' with the stars to be good company.

BILL.  I have a *ro-man-tic* soul, I have.

JIM.  Yeh  It *roams* when they's work to be done.

BILL.  *(With a far-away look)*  Prob'ly they's enough paper in there so's we won't have to do another job for six months.  We might even go South for the Winter

JIM.  Say, was you visitin' in Chinatown to-day? Come down to earth!  *(He goes to work.  BILL sits in chair at left of the table and places his feet on table.)*

BILL.  Jim.

JIM.  Yeh?

BILL  If—if they should be a nice li'l sparkler

in there—say one or two carats—what would look
nice in a tiffany settin', can I have it?

JIM. *(Dropping his tools)*  Now I *know* this here
combine is headed for the bottom.  When you get so
sweet on a dame that you begin thinkin' 'bout givin'
her a rock, it's time to dissolve partnership.

BILL.  You got me wrong, all wrong.  Honest you
have, Jim.

JIM.  Like hake I have!

BILL.  I was just thinkin' that we ought to be
grateful to the maid who chattered about this place.'

JIM.  She didn't know what you was.  She didn't
suspect that she was givin' a second-story a tip.

BILL.  I know.  It was just passin' conversation
But, Jim, I feel as if we owed her somethin' for it.

JIM.  Forget it.

BILL.  Honest, after the haul we're goin' to make,
my conscience will bother me if she don't get a re-
ward.  I pass her real often when I take my airin'
in the park.

JIM.  Walk somewheres else, then.  *(He throws
a pair of pliers to the center of the room.)*  Here,
stop your moonin' long enough to fix the 'phone.

BILL.  But I'm lookout on this job; I've got to
keep a-listenin'.

JIM.  You don't have to cut the wires with your
ears, do you?  If you can't do two things to once
now, you'll be doin' it later.

BILL.  I don't get you.

JIM.  You'll be doin' time and breakin' stone to
once.

BILL.  All right.  *(He leisurely gets the pliers,
crawls under the table and cuts the wire; then throws
the pliers on the table.)*  There, now I can listen
again.  *(He dusts his hands, slouches into the chair
again, pulls his hat down to shade his eyes, and
sighs.)*

JIM. *(Working on the safe)* Did that job exhaust you?

BILL. I stood the shock well.

JIM. What you blowin' off steam for, then?

BILL. I was sympathizin' with you. That's a tough one.

JIM. Thanks. It helps a lot. *(He works in silence several seconds. BILL is quiet, but suddenly he starts.)*

BILL. Cheese it  Here comes old paralysis. I heard his wagon squeak.

*(JIM hastily shoves the tools under the safe and hides behind the screen up right. BILL conceals himself in the curtains of the upper window  BENSON, a young fellow dressed in a business suit, opens the doors, turns all the lights on, and wheels in MR. HEMIT on a chaise-longue of wicker, which is mounted on wheels so that HEMIT'S elbows are about on a level with the top of the table. HEMIT is attired in a dressing-gown.)*

HEMIT. Now get me just right, Benson. I want the light directly over my head.

BENSON. Yes, sir.

HEMIT. Last evening you left me too far back, and it shone in my eyes.

BENSON. How is that, sir? *(He wheels HEMIT under the light, within reach of the table.)*

HEMIT. Good. Very good. *(BENSON gets the small table and places it at HEMIT'S right; then he places the music rack just below the table.)*

BENSON. Will you smoke, sir?

HEMIT. One of those little cigars. *(BENSON clips the cigar, places it between HEMIT'S lips, and*

*lights it.  Then he places a magazine on the rack.)*
Not that one; the other.  (BENSON *exchanges magazines.)*
  BENSON.  Where were you reading?
  HEMIT.  I don't remember.  I wrote it on the
cover.
  BENSON.  *(Inspecting cover)*  Page 296.  *(He
opens and places it on rack; then swings telephone
toward* HEMIT.*)*
  HEMIT.  Oh, Benson, will you see that a head-
piece is put on that 'phone?  It annoys and tires me
to hold the receiver to my ear.
  BENSON.  I shall attend to it the first thing in the
morning  Are you comfortable now?
  HEMIT.  Yes, I guess so.  *(He sees the pliers and
picks them up.)*  Benson, to whom do these belong?
What are they doing here?

*(JIM, who is carefully observing everything from
    behind the screen, is tense.  He shakes his fist
    in BILL's direction.)*

  BENSON.  I don't know, sir.
  HEMIT.  That's funny.
  BENSON.  Oh, the repair man must have left them
here this afternoon.

*(JIM relaxes with relief.)*

  HEMIT  Take them away; they don't make a
handsome ornament.
  BENSON.  Yes, sir.  *(He takes them.)*  I shall re-
turn at the usual time; just as soon as school is out.
  HEMIT.  It is very commendable that you wish to
get ahead enough to spend your evenings in school
after working all day.

BENSON. Thank you, sir. Good-bye

HEMIT. Good-bye, Benson. (BENSON *starts for the door.*) Oh, Benson, I could stand a little more fresh air. Open the window a trifle wider.

BENSON. Yes, sir. (*He nearly reaches the window where* BILL *is concealed.* JIM *holds his breath in fear.*)

HEMIT. (*Glancing over his shoulder*) Not that one. The other. (BENSON *adjusts the indicated window, turns out the wall lights, and exits, closing the door.*) Not a thing to do now but take it easy. (*He reads for several moments; then, as he turns a page, the magazine falls from the rack to the floor.*) Confound it! Just my luck! (JIM *steps from behind the screen. His face is now hidden from the eyes down by a black handkerchief, and his hat is pulled well down over his eyes.*)

JIM Allow me, sir.

HEMIT. (*Startled*) Who the devil are you? Where did you come from?

JIM. (*Picking up magazine*) Let's see, page 296, wasn't it? (*He opens the magazine and places it in position*)

HEMIT. How did you get in? What do you want?

JIM. I want to keep you from getting lonely, and for amusement we will open this. (*He pulls tools from under safe.*)

HEMIT. (*Alarmed*) You're a burglar!

JIM. You're clever! How'd you guess it?

HEMIT. How long have you been here?

JIM. (*Getting to work on the safe*) Not long enough. What time *did* we come in, Bill?

BILL (*Stepping out; his features also concealed*) Search me.

HEMIT. Two of you!

JIM Sure. Had to bring my little pal along—

just to make it a nice party.   It really doesn't take two to clean out a paralyzed man's safe.

BILL.   *(Pompously)*   I can carry on the conversation while Cicero is carving his way to the contents of that can.

JIM.   I could do it better if I had more light on the subject.   We don't need to keep things so dark, now that we have had an understanding.

BILL.   It would be better than the flashlight.   *(He sits at left of table.)*   Why don't you put 'em on, Cicero?

JIM.   You lazy piece of humanity.   You pull the window-shades, anyway.   If anyone looked over from the hotel they might take a notion to join this masquerade party.   *(He turns on lights as BILL obeys.)*

HEMIT.   Hm!   Guess I won't have such a quiet evening after all.   *(He lays his cigar in the ash-tray.)*

JIM.   Don't let us disturb you in the least.   I'll be as quiet as possible, and Algy there would rather sleep than talk.   He's the laziest man you ever saw.

HEMIT.   Is that so?

JIM.   Yeh.   He gets up at five o'clock in the mornin' so's to have more time to loaf.   *(He drills )*

BILL.   Aw, stow the chatter, Cicero.   *(He puts his feet on the table )*

HEMIT.   I should think that he would be an encumbrance to you.

BILL.   Sometimes he thinks I am, but I collect lots o' valuable information for him.

HEMIT.   Really?

BILL.   Yeh.   F'r instance, I gathered the dope about you bein' a paralytic, and about the amount o' stuff you always have around.

HEMIT.   You don't say.

BILL.   Yeh.   And I've been a-watchin' you every

night for a week—from across the street with field-glasses.

JIM. Here now, Algy, don't give away the secrets of the profession.

BILL. I just want to prove to the gentleman that I ain't so black as you paint me or as this silk makes me look. I'm a good feller, I am

HEMIT. I guess you are, both of you, or you would just pull your guns and force me to give you the combination of the safe.

JIM. That's where you have us wrong, Cap. We don't carry no firearms. We don't believe in 'em.

HEMIT How thoughtful of you.

BILL. *(Half asleep)* Yeh If we ever gets nabbed it makes a lot of difference to the judge whether or not we pack gats.

JIM We're thoughtful, all right. *(He straightens up.)* Say, this is as tough as any I ever did.

HEMIT. Do you think you will succeed very soon?

JIM She's liable to open any moment now

HEMIT. The combination is written on that card on top of the safe.

BILL. *(Sitting upright)* What!

JIM. Quit your kiddin'!

HEMIT. Too bad you overlooked it.

BILL. Is he givin' straight dope?

JIM *(Gets card)* It looks like a combination.

HEMIT. It is. And it *used* to open that safe.

JIM. Wha' d'ye mean, used to?

HEMIT. In fact, it did until this noon. I opened it at eleven o'clock, took something out, and then locked it out of habit. An hour later I tried to open it and couldn't.

JIM *(On his knees, card in hand)* I'll soon have it. I'm an expert.

HEMIT And this afternoon I had an expert from

the Hosler Safe Company come up, and he couldn't budge it.

JIM. What? Well, I'm no better than they are. *(Drops card and gets busy with drill)*

HEMIT So you see you are doing me a very great service if you succeed in opening it.

JIM. We'll succeed very soon.

BILL. We like to be of service.

HEMIT. Do you?

BILL. Sure thing.

HEMIT Then perhaps you will open the drawer on the other side of this table and give me that box of cigars you will see.

BILL. All right *(He takes out the box without rising)* Gosh, it's heavy. Are they trick cigars?

HEMIT. *(Watching him closely)* It is almost a full box.

BILL *(Shoves the box across the table with his foot)* There y'are.

(HEMIT attempts to get it, but it is just beyond his reach.)

HEMIT. Can you give it another inch in this direction?

BILL *(Stretching his leg with great effort to reach it)* There. Must be hell to be as helpless as you are.

JIM. *(At work)* You're darn near as bad, Algy, old dear.

BILL. Aw, that record's cracked, Cicero. Put on another.

HEMIT. *(Placing box on small table)* Thanks— oh, I needn't have bothered you. I forgot this one *(Relights his cigar.)*

BILL. *(With a groan)* All that effort for nothin'.

JIM. *(Viciously tugging at the safe door)* Effort! What are you doin' that takes any effort?

BILL. Don't strain yourself, Cis, old kid.

JIM. I won't. Just about ten seconds more and we can take the sardines out o' this can.

BILL. *(Licking his lips)* Um-m-m-m!

HEMIT. You don't know how I shall appreciate it if you succeed.

BILL. Don't worry, we'll do it.

HEMIT. There's something in it I need very badly.

BILL. I hope you don't need what we do, brother I'm afraid that we will have to be impolite enough to take first choice.

JIM. *(Tapping the combination and pulling it; with a hard pull the door swings open.)* Ah! Here we are!

BILL. *(Hurrying over)* Fine!

HEMIT Great!

JIM. *(Pulls out a drawer)* Empty. *(He throws it aside and takes another.)* So's this one! *(Rapidly pulls them all out.)*

BILL. Well, I'll be darned!

JIM. The whole bloomin' thing is empty!

HEMIT. *(Sternly, tapping the cigar-box)* But this isn't. *(They turn.)*

BILL. And I handed it to you! I had the kale and didn't know it. *(He steps toward HEMIT, who quickly opens the box and draws out an automatic revolver with which he covers them )*

HEMIT. And *this* isn't empty! There are three apiece, and one extra for the first gentleman who moves.

BILL. *(Stunned)* You old rascal!

HEMIT. *(Amiably)* I suppose I'm expected to use the phrases they always do in books, so here goes: "Hands up," gentlemen. *(They mechanically obey.)*

JIM.  After all my work——
BILL.  I told you to soup it.
HEMIT.  *(Opening the wooden box on the large table, and displaying a roll of bills and numerous articles of jewelry.)*  This is what I took out of the safe this morning.  Is it what you were after?
BILL.  Oh, what a roll!  And it was right under my heels all the time.
HEMIT.  It's too much bother to write checks; easier to hand over money; so I'm my own banker.
JIM.  He's almost as lazy as you are, Algy.
BILL.  Why did you want us to open the safe?
HEMIT  Well, you see, I accidentally locked my dyspepsia tablets in there and I need one right now.
JIM.  Wouldn't that make you sick!

(HEMIT *takes up the telephone receiver.)*

BILL.  That won't work.
HEMIT.  I hardly expected it would.
JIM.  Well, are you goin' to sit there and keep us covered until your man gets back?
HEMIT.  *(Languidly)*  Dear me, no.  That would be too tiresome.
BILL.  What are you goin' to do?
HEMIT.  *(With a sigh)*  I'm nicely settled, but I'll have to escort you downstairs to a policeman *(Keeping them covered, he leisurely swings his feet to the floor and rises.  JIM and BILL are dumbfounded.)*
JIM.  You, Bill!  I thought he couldn't walk!
BILL.  S'help me, I thought he was paralyzed!
HEMIT.  *(Points to the ceiling)*  The paralyzed man lives on the next floor.  *(He yawns)*
BILL.  Then what—what—— *(He points to the place from which HEMIT has risen)*  You've been in that every evenin' this week!
HEMIT.  *(Stretching his free arm, with another*

*yawn)*  I'm perfectly healthy, but I believe in taking it as easy as I can.  Go along.  *(He motions them toward the door.)*

JIM.  *(With a quiet laugh)*  You've lost the honor, Bill.

BILL.  What honor?

JIM.  Of bein' the laziest man in the world.


CURTAIN

## TAKE HER, SHE'S MINE
Phoebe and Henry Ephron

*Comedy / 11m, 6f / Various Sets*
Art Carney and Phyllis Thaxter played the Broadway roles of parents of two typical American girls enroute to college. The story is based on the wild and wooly experiences the authors had with their daughters, Nora Ephron and Delia Ephron, themselves now well known writers. The phases of a girl's life are cause for enjoyment except to fearful fathers. Through the first two years, the authors tell us, college girls are frightfully sophisticated about all departments of human life. Then they pass into the "liberal" period of causes and humanitarianism, and some into the intellectual lethargy of beatniksville. Finally, they start to think seriously of their lives as grown ups. It's an experience in growing up, as much for the parents as for the girls.

"A warming comedy. A delightful play about parents vs kids. It's loaded with laughs. It's going to be a smash hit."
*– New York Mirror*

## MURDER AMONG FRIENDS
### Bob Barry

*Comedy thriller / 4m, 2f / Interior*

Take an aging, exceedingly vain actor; his very rich wife; a double dealing, double loving agent, plunk them down in an elegant New York duplex and add dialogue crackling with wit and laughs, and you have the basic elements for an evening of pure, sophisticated entertainment. Angela, the wife and Ted, the agent, are lovers and plan to murder Palmer, the actor, during a contrived robbery on New Year's Eve. But actor and agent are also lovers and have an identical plan to do in the wife. A murder occurs, but not one of the planned ones.

"Clever, amusing, and very surprising."
– *New York Times*

"A slick, sophisticated show that is modern and very funny."
– WABC TV

# THE BIRTHDAY PARTY
Harold Pinter

*Drama / 4m, 2f / Interior*

In a small house at a coastal resort live a man, his mentally wayward wife and their boarder who has been with them for a year. He is a strange chap, unkempt and in flight from we know not what. Enter an even stranger sleek Jewish man and his muscle bound Irish henchman. The mentally immature wife accommodates them with a room and then decides that it is time for the boarder to have a birthday. At the party she arranges, the new guests play cruel games with the boarder, break his glasses, make a buffoon of him, and push him over the psychotic precipice. The next morning he is reduced to a gibbering idiot and meekly leaves with them.

"Fascinating capacity to be menacing, ominous and evocative of some dark and threatening doom."
– *New York Post*

"The most interesting play to be seen on Broadway."
– *New York Times*